IRISH NIGHTS

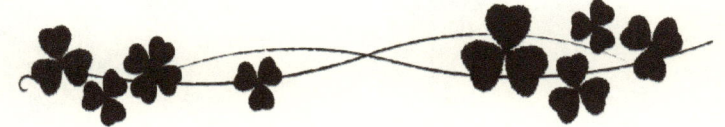

Marissa Dobson

&

Thomas Dobson

To everyone who supported us along the way.

CHAPTER ONE

In Dublin, Ireland for more than a week and the only thing Joslynn Ashburn had seen was the inside of the hotel and now this dark pub. This wasn't how the trip was supposed to turn out. It had been intended as a romantic getaway with a little work on the side, but it ended up being full of work and zero romance. The moments she had with Sal were few and far between and when she did see him, there was nothing fun about it. If anything, the experience was teetering on the edge of violent.

A breath caught in her lungs as the pub door opened. Fearful it was Sal, she scooted further into the booth, hoping the darkness from the pub would keep her hidden. A couple walked in, locked in an embrace.

Seeing them together made her long for what they appeared to have. But, reality had already shown her that relationships were not always what they seemed, and even though the couple appeared to be happy, there might be dark secrets hiding beneath the surface.

"Hey there, lass."

Lost in her thoughts about relationships and couples, she hadn't noticed one of the guys from the bar had moseyed up to her table. As she turned her attention to him, she caught the pungent aroma of alcohol rolling off him in waves. The scent was so strong she would have thought he'd bathed in it, but from the way he could barely stay upright, she had no doubt that he'd drunk it.

Not wanting to cause any problems, she kept quiet and took the man in. His dark hair was shaggy, nearly reaching his ears, and his jaw was covered with a day's growth, giving him a more unkempt appearance. Something about the way he looked at her made her heart race and her chest tighten.

"Let me buy you a drink and get to know you."

"I…um…." Needing a place to hide and get out of the rain until she could figure out what to do, she didn't want any issues. Telling this guy to get lost could bring unnecessary attention to her sitting in the dark corner, nursing a soda. Yet, allowing him to join her would lead him on.

"Come on." The man stepped closer and leaned down toward her. "A young lass like yourself alone in a bar—what else could you be looking for?"

"I'm…"

"Back off." A deep, gruff voice cut through the thick air between them.

"Screw you man, I was here first."

"Doubt that." He slipped into the booth next to her and slipped his arm around her shoulder. "Hey babe, sorry I'm late."

Her eyes widened as she stared at the man sitting beside her. His appearance might have changed since the last time she'd seen him but there was no doubt that voice belonged to her brother's best friend, Chip Olson. As the sound of her own heartbeat filled her ears, their gazes locked on one another. With every blink, she realized he was actually there in front of her, but she still couldn't believe her eyes. How had he found her?

"What the hell?"

Chip turned his attention back to the other man. "Get lost. My fiancée and I have plans."

The man stumbled back, mumbling something Joslynn didn't catch. As he did she turned to face Chip, whose arm stayed around her shoulders.

"What are you doing here? How did you know I was here?" A couple of months had passed since she'd seen him and it looked as if he'd spent most of that time in the gym. For as long as she had known him he'd always been toned, yet now his muscles were more defined.

"Your cell phone."

"What?" The question came out louder than she expected, causing the bartender to glance in their direction.

"Yesterday…hell, it might have been the day before with the time difference. I don't know." He glanced around the dark bar as if he was looking for someone. "I stopped by your apartment and Annie was there. She told me what was happening."

"She told you." Even as disbelief bubbled within her, she knew she shouldn't be surprised. Annie and Chip were cousins and they were close. She would have confided in him without thinking anything about it. "Still that doesn't explain why you're here or why you hacked my cell phone to find me. How is that even possible?"

"Friends," he stated as if it explained everything. "Come on, let's go somewhere else."

"Ah…" She wasn't even sure why she tried to argue. What was she going to say? Instead, she grabbed her bag and followed him as he rose from the booth. Guilt coursed through her as realization dawned on her. *If Chip's here, Jack knows.*

Being deployed, her brother could be in a dangerous territory and the last thing she wanted was to be the reason his head wasn't in the action. If he got hurt because of her, she'd never be able to forgive herself. *Stay safe Jack.*

After Chip stepped off the plane, the only thing he wanted was a stiff drink but the moment he walked into the bar and found Joslynn sitting there, the need for alcohol disappeared. All he could think about was getting her out of there to somewhere safe. The way the guy watched them, even after Chip had told him she was his fiancée, unnerved him. The darkened atmosphere made it harder for him to see everything and played havoc with his already deteriorated vision. They needed to make their exit before the alcohol could give the other man any stupid ideas.

Leading her out of the bar, he made sure to keep his arm on her. He wanted to say that it was all part of playing his role as fiancé. Though, if he was honest with himself, he didn't want to let go of her. The concern and anger that rushed through him when he heard of her situation had drove him to the brink as he made his way across the ocean to her.

Outside the rain had begun to fall again, making him wish he'd brought a jacket with him. Without one, he used it as an excuse to keep her close. Drawing her tight against his body, he guided her down the sidewalk in the direction he'd come from only minutes before.

"Where are we going?"

"I got a hotel room. It's just up the street."

"Hotel room." She stumbled as she looked up at him.

"It's a place we can talk. Then you can…" He wasn't sure what he was going to say. Go back to that asshole? No, that wasn't an option.

"Can what?" she pushed.

"Anything you want, Jos. Anything." *Except go back to him.*

Between the rain and the late hour, the roads were clear. Still, he scanned the area looking for any threats. Even as a civilian, he wasn't able to stop. His training had kept him alive while overseas and now, even with his injuries, he was still in warrior mode. *They took me out of the fight, but they can't take the fight out of me.*

That thought had gotten him through months of rehab and had somehow became his motto to live by. He wasn't giving up and he wasn't about to allow Jos to give up, either. Even in the dim light of the bar he could see she was cracked from what had happened, but he wasn't going to allow it to break her. He'd do what he could to pull her through it, just like she had done for him. She didn't know how much her messages to him after his accident had meant to him, but it was time to show her. She had been his rock and now he'd return the favor.

CHAPTER TWO

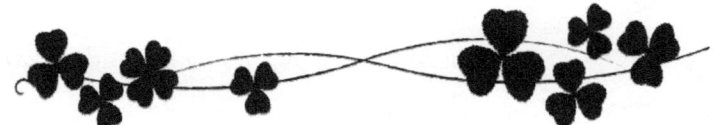

Sitting in the hotel room, Joslynn still couldn't believe Chip was with her. The one person—besides her brother—she'd wished was by her side was now actually there. It still felt like a dream, one she didn't want to wake up from. Even though he hated flying, he'd gotten on a plane and flew across the world to find her. That was the kind of man she wanted to make her life with. Not a man like Sal, who only cared about appearances and money. There was so much more to life than money and status. Those were the things she wanted in her life.

"Drink?" Chip stood next to the in-room bar, his hand already untwisting one of the little liquor bottles.

"I'm fine." She dropped her bag onto the floor and sank down onto the arm chair. "Want to tell me why you're here yet?"

"I already told you, Annie told me what was happening."

"Yeah, you told me that." She glanced around the large hotel room. "That doesn't explain why you flew half way around the world."

"I'd fly to the end of the universe for you." Without bothering with a glass, he tipped the small liquor bottle back, chugging half of it. "You don't believe I'd do nothing, do you?"

She wasn't sure how to answer his question, so she threw a question of her own at him. "What did Annie tell you? I mean…"

"That the asshole was harassing you. That your boss forced his jerk of a son on you if you wanted to keep your job." Sitting the bottle on the bar top, he stalked toward her. "Fuck, Jos, what were you thinking? Jack would kill the guy if he knew."

"If…" That one word gave her hope that Jack didn't know what was currently happening.

"You thought I've spoken to him." He let out a sigh and squatted down in front of her. "Even if I had spoken to him, what would I have told him? That you were in Ireland with this asshole, and in trouble? How do you think that would have gone? Without him able to do anything to help, it would have only distracted him."

She reached out and closed the distance between them by placing her hand over his. "Thank you."

"I have to say I was surprised to find you in that bar instead of his hotel room. So why don't you tell me what else has happened?"

As she leaned back in the chair, her hand slid off his. Yet, she barely noticed the loss of touch. Rather, her thoughts were filled with what had brought her to Dublin. *Accompany Sal on this trip and perform whatever duties he needs. With a satisfactory report from him, we'll discuss the promotion when you return.*

"It's been a disaster from the start." She shook her head and looked back up to meet his gaze. "You know what? I'll have that drink. Anything strong."

"Coming right up." He rose from his seat in front of her and headed back to the bar.

"I never thought things would turn out like this. I mean I wasn't sure about this trip or spending the time alone here with Sal. Without his dad to keep him in check, he's a different person." She'd recognized the signs before but until this trip she hadn't realized how bad things were between them. Nor had she realized how dangerous things had become. Not just to her, but Sal was also a threat to himself and those around him, especially women.

"This trip was supposed to be my key to the promotion. Instead, it left me without a job and a ticket home." She accepted the glass he held out to her and before continuing, she took a sip. The burn of the alcohol as it slid down her throat warmed her and gave her the courage she needed to tell him what had happened.

"Sal's an asshole, there's no denying that, but I never expected him to go this far. What he was asking…" Her checks heated with embarrassment at the thought of telling him about the straw that broke the camel's back and sent her running from Sal's hotel room. "Even though I knew it would cost me my job, I couldn't go through with it. But I never thought he'd tell me to find my own way home. He has the plane tickets."

"Don't worry about that. I've got us booked on a flight out in two days. Do you have your passport?"

"It's in my purse." She nodded. "I'll pay you back. I swear."

"Jos." Leaning from his seat, he took her hand in his. "It's not the money and that's not why I came here. You should have called me."

"I couldn't. I thought you'd tell Jack. Plus, what was I going to say?"

"Damn it, Jos." His hand tightened over hers, squeezing it tightly. "You know me better than that. You know I'd be there for you."

"I couldn't risk it getting back to Jack. Not when I had other options. I was waiting for Annie to get back to me. I just needed to find the money to get a ticket home. Once I got there, I'd be able to pay them back. I have the money in my checking account. I just never wanted to deal with credit cards and my bank card was stolen before I left Pittsburgh. All I'm left with is the cash I have on me. It shouldn't have been a problem; everything was supposed to go on the business card, but…"

"That jackass has it, which leaves you at his mercy." Chip's voice held a deepness to it that hadn't been there before. He was angry and it was seeping into his tone.

"Can't really blame him." She shrugged. "It's his father's company."

"Don't stand up for that asshole." He rose again, his hand still holding hers, and pulled her up to stand with him. "Did you really think Jack or I would stand by and let you marry that imbecile?"

"You?" Her eyebrow rose in question as she wondered if she was reading more into what he was saying than she should be.

"You're too smart to act as if you haven't known." He pulled her tight against the front of his body as his hand slid along her ribcage.

Air escaped from between her teeth as pain blossomed within her stomach. The slightest brush of his hand against the fresh bruises along her side made her woozy.

"What the hell?" He stepped back, his fingers gripping the edge of her sweater and pulling it up before she could stop him.

"It's nothing."

"Nothing!" he roared, his gaze on the bruise that ran from the middle of her ribcage down the length of her side until it disappeared below the waistband of her jeans. "He did this to you."

"Chip." She reached up to cup his cheek. Her fingers brushed along the stumble.

"She told me he threatened you. That he wanted you to do something you weren't comfortable with. But she didn't tell me he put his hands on you."

She could see the fires of rage burning within his eyes. "Annie didn't know. I didn't want her to worry."

"Never again." His fingertips brushed along the edges of the bruises. "In the morning, I'll go to the hotel and get your suitcase. After that you will have no further contact with him."

"No." As his gaze shoot up to hers, her chest tightened.

"What?"

"Just forget the suitcase. Nothing that's there is important." She slipped her hand out from his and brought it to his chest. "You said I should have known I could have counted on you. Well, just as I knew that, I also was aware what you'd want to do to him. Don't…please, Chip. It's not worth it."

"You're worth it." He placed his hand over hers. "No man should ever lay a hand on a woman."

"I just want to forget it all. To go home." She turned her hand around, so she could intertwine their fingers. "You can't be there for me if you get yourself locked up in Ireland. Please, Chip."

"Fuck!" He stepped back from her. "I'm going to grab some food. Stay here."

"Chip—"

He held up his hand, cutting her off. "I need some air and we both need to eat. You have my word, I'm not going to hunt him down *tonight*."

Knowing that was the best she was going to get from him, she let it drop. Chip and Jack had always been hot headed. Both of them had strong principals and would stand up for what they believed was right. Maybe that was why they'd both joined the military.

As Chip stood in the diner across the street waiting for the takeout he ordered, he did his best to battle his emotions. He wanted to hunt down that asshole and teach him a lesson for touching her. *No one touches what's mine.* Even as the thought flashed across his mind, he knew he had no claim over her. Still, that didn't diminish his need to teach this asshole a lesson.

Men like Sal would feed off whoever was easiest and until he had to pay the price for his actions, he wouldn't stop. With his father riding to the rescue every time there was the hint of scandal it would be hard to get Sal to see the error of his ways. Chip would need to find the opportunity to confront the bastard when he was alone. Though Jos was right, that needed to wait until they were back in the States. Back home, he'd have the upper hand. He just needed to keep his temper in check until the right opportunity appeared.

Patience had never been his strong suit. The only trait that outranked his patience was his inability to take orders. Funny how he'd lasted eight years in the military doing the two things he hated most—waiting and taking orders. He'd still be following his commanders if it wasn't for his last unfortunate mission.

"Sir." A waitress strolled toward him with a brown paper bag in hand. "Your food. Enjoy."

"Thank you." He accepted the bag and headed for the door.

There would be plenty of time to put a game plan together. For now, he wanted to get back to Jos. He needed to show her that she deserved better than Sal. Hell, she deserved better than him but they had two days before their flight back to the States; in this time, he planned to show her just how much she meant to him.

CHAPTER THREE

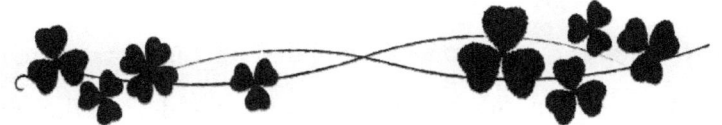

Joslynn lost track of how many times she paced past the windows in Chip's hotel room. Each time she scanned the sidewalk below looking for any sign of him but from the height, she couldn't make out any features. Every person below looked like a small dot.

"Where are you, Chip?"

Her cell phone beeped, as if answering her. Except it wasn't from him. Annie's name popped up on the screen with a text. *Just got off work. Everything okay?*

Okay? Nothing seemed to be okay at the moment. For a brief instant when Chip had found her in the bar, she'd thought everything would be fine, but now she wasn't sure. He was out there somewhere. Even with his word that he wouldn't go in search of Sal, it didn't mean the two of them couldn't bump into each other. If that happened, there'd be no stopping Chip. He was too headstrong, just like her brother. Between the two of them, she had cleaned enough wounds to last her a lifetime. That was one of the reasons why she hadn't followed in her mother's footsteps and become a nurse.

Did you know Chip was coming? She pressed send before she could rethink her question. With Chip in Dublin there was no reason to worry Annie with what had happened. There was also no reason to tell her that Chip might be out there walking the streets in search of Sal. She could fill her best friend in once she got back home.

I told him about Sal but didn't think he'd show up. Did it cause another big fight with you and Sal?

She stared down at her phone, debating how to answer that question. *Long story. Sal and I are done. Staying with Chip until we fly home. I'll fill you in then.* She hit the send button as her gaze turned back to the street.

As always with her, her thoughts conjured up the worst outcomes to any possible situation. If Chip didn't come back, she would be in the same position she had been in hours before. Only now one less option of help was out there for her to call. Actually, it would eliminate two options. If Chip ended up in an Irish jail because of her, she couldn't ask Annie for the money to help her get home. Not after she became the reason her cousin ended up behind bars.

"Deep breath. It's going to be fine." Even saying the words aloud didn't stop the anxiety from rising within her. Everything seemed to slam into her at once until she felt as though she was drowning in all of the bad shit that had happened.

Sinking down onto the small sofa near the window, she brought her hands up to her face. Squeezing the bridge of her nose, she tried to push her tears away. Everything was crashing into her and she couldn't handle it. She wanted to be back home and put all of this behind her.

The hotel room door opened, and Chip stood in the entryway. "I'm back."

She ran her fingers under her eyes, drying up any tears that escaped. "Thank Heaven." She let out a sigh of relief.

"The lobby clerk recommended shepherd's pie from the diner across the street. I guess it's their weekly special." He held up a brown paper bag. "I hope that's okay with you."

"It's fine." Even though she wanted to rise from the sofa and go to him to put her arms around him, she forced herself to stay where she was. This was

Chip, her brother's best friend. She couldn't allow her emotions to get a hold of her so much that she forgot this. No matter what she felt for him, she couldn't allow herself to get carried away.

"While you were gone, Annie texted. You didn't tell her you were coming?"

"No." Sitting the bag on the small two-person dining table, he began to pull out the food. "It was a spur of the moment decision."

"Spur of the moment? Really?" She moved over to the table so that she was standing next to him. "This isn't like you just got into your truck and all of a sudden ended up at my door. You flew to Ireland to see me."

"True." He sat two bottles of water on the table and tossed the bag aside. "I found myself sitting outside the airport, debating what to do. At that time, I wasn't sure if you needed me or if I was overreacting. I did know I was going to have words with your asshole boss and his son when you returned. But I wasn't sure it was necessary to come here and possibly embarrass you."

"What made you go into the airport?" Uneasy, she focused her attention on the task at hand and took the lid off the to-go containers.

"You, Jos." His finger brushed along the curve of her face until he reached her jaw and gently he tugged her head up to look at him. "From what Annie told me I could tell how upset you were. I couldn't sit by and do nothing. Even if all that happened was that I come here on the pretense of business and offered you a little comfort."

"That's a long way to go to offer comfort." As she stared up at him, their gazes locked.

"There's no distance I wouldn't go for you."

His words tightened her chest until she thought she couldn't draw another breath. She didn't want to read further into what he said but her heart told her to trust her instincts. She moved close to him. Their chests brushed against each other as they breathed. "Tell me I'm wrong. Tell me I'm reading into this."

He slipped his arm around her and pressed his hand against the small of her back, drawing her even closer to him. "Is that what you want? Or do you want to see where this could take us?"

Us. That single word sent her heartrate into overdrive. *What about Jack?* The thought of her brother slammed into her, but she couldn't stop herself from rising up to press her lips to his.

Butterflies danced within her stomach as their lips met. She looped her arms around his neck to gain some balance as his tongue slipped between her lips. The kiss she meant to be sweet blossomed into passion. Until that moment, she never understood it when her mother would tell her that during the first kiss with her father, fireworks exploded, and she knew he was the one. Now it was as if the grand finale was lit within her.

As the kiss ended, she leaned against him, her thoughts hazy while she tried to digest what had just happened. This was the moment she had been waiting for but there was still a huge ball of concern in her stomach. Going down this road with Chip could mean the end of their friendship. If things didn't work out, it wouldn't just ruin things between them but would also affect things among the four of them—she, Chip, Annie, and Jack. They had been almost inseparable all of their lives. Now, if they went through with this, they'd throw a curve ball into their friendships.

As much as she wanted to explore what might be happening between them, she wasn't sure she could risk that. He was one of her best friends and the thought of losing him hurt her like a stab in the heart.

CHAPTER FOUR

With his arms around her, holding her tight against him, Chip watched as she worked through what had just happened. He almost expected her to pull away from him, to shut him out. Instead, she took comfort in his embrace. Even without asking, he knew she was thinking about her brother and Annie. Their friendship meant a lot to both of them and this could put a strain on it. Said friendship had been the reason he'd kept his feelings to himself for so long, but that time was gone.

She deserved someone better than him, but that knowledge didn't stop him from wanting to claim her as his own. He couldn't allow that knowledge to sidetrack him because he knew what it was like to lose her. When he learned she was engaged to Sal he thought he'd lost her for good. But now, the door he believed closed was open, so he had to try.

"Don't overthink it, Jos." He pressed his lips to the top of her head.

"Jack and Annie—"

"This isn't about them." He leaned back to look down at her. "This is about us."

"Bull. Ever since kindergarten we've always been a foursome. What do you think they'll say when they find out? You're Jack's best friend. What do you think he'll do when he finds out you're sleeping with his sister?"

"I'm planning on more than sleeping." He ran his hand down her arm, caressing her. "Jos, I can't tell you when it happened because it feels like it's been this way forever, but you're the woman who's filled every fantasy of mine. The one who occupies my dreams at night. The strength that I needed to keep fighting after coming home from my tour of duty, burned and damaged. I understand if you want someone…unscarred, but don't use Jack and Annie as the reason. Be honest."

"Unscarred…" She shook her head. "That never crossed my mind. Your scars take nothing away from you. If anything, they add to you."

"Bullshit!" His tone was deeper than he'd meant for it to be but still, she didn't pull away from him.

"Okay, maybe I'm wrong. They did take something…" As he started to pull away, she grabbed hold of his arm, her fingers pressing into the scars from the burns on his arm. "They took skin. Nothing more. They don't make you less of the person you were before. They show what kind of man you truly are."

She pushed up the long sleeve of his T-shirt, revealing his forearm and the beginning of the burns that laced their way up his arm and across his torso. "These scars show that you're a man who would risk everything to save someone. You ran into a burning building to save that little girl and a fellow soldier. Everyone else was escaping the inferno but not you."

As her fingers traced along the burns, his thoughts were pulled back into the past. After hours on the plane with the horrors of the past pressing on him, the last thing he wanted to do was revisit them again. Those memories held nothing but horror and sadness and brought the need for a stiff drink back to him. Only one drink wouldn't be enough. He'd need a bottle of liquor to push the past away this time.

"You don't believe me."

Her soft words brought him back from his thoughts and into the moment. He wanted to wrap his arms around her, to bring her back against his chest and take comfort in her the same way she took comfort in him. Instead of giving in to his desire, though, he glanced down at her hand as she traced along each of the burns. The tender touch lit something inside him that he couldn't put into words.

"What if all my actions did was cause more pain and suffering?" The question was out before he could stop himself. Never before had he voiced his concern and he hadn't meant to now.

"I know you went through some rough patches when you came home—"

"I wasn't talking about that." He shook his head. "Forget I said anything."

"The little girl." Her hand stilled over his arm and she looked up at him. "Jack told me she'd lost her leg from where it was crushed under the pillar that collapsed on her, but she survived."

In the blink of an eye, he was taken back. Not to his tour of duty, or the weeks in the hospital recovering from his injuries, but to the letter he'd received that had ultimately led him to Ireland. He could see himself standing in his kitchen with the small silver cross in his hand.

I found this on E.

The letter had been short and to the point. He already knew about the attack on her village and the injuries she'd sustained. It had happened weeks before, but the news had been sketchy at best. He held out hope that she was strong enough to get through it but that hope had been destroyed in one short sentence.

"Chip." Her fingers tightened around his arm until her fingernails pressed into the skin. "Chip!"

"Huh?" He opened his eyes to look at her and the concern etched on her face sliced through him. He had been so lost in his own torment, he hadn't realized she had been calling to him. "I'm fine."

"You're not, but you will be." She slipped her hand into his, interlocking

23

their fingers, and pulled him toward the bed. "Come here."

"What about the food?"

"It will be there." She let go of his hand and crawled up onto the king bed. Pressing her back against the headboard, she tapped the space beside her. "You don't have to tell me anything you don't want to but come here."

His lips curled up into a smile as he slipped onto the bed next to her. "This is why I went to your apartment. I hoped you wouldn't mind me showing up unannounced because I needed this."

"I never mind when you show up." She curled against his body, and he wrapped his arm around her shoulders, bringing her closer.

"After I opened the envelope, I didn't know what I was doing…everything was hazy. One minute I was standing in my kitchen and the next I was knocking on your door. The only thing I could think of was seeing you. I didn't want to talk; I just wanted to turn on some movie or television, order a pizza, and hold you in my arms. Whatever was going on inside of my head, I knew that it would settle the moment you were next to me. Just like it did whenever you'd visit me at the hospital."

"I'm sorry I wasn't there." She looped her arm over his waist and rested her head on his chest, just as she always did when they'd curl up together.

"Don't apologize." Needing to see more of her, he reached over to push her dark brown hair back from her face. "Right here, right now, this is what gives me confidence in moving forward with us."

She tipped her head to look up at him. "Sometimes I feel as if we bounce around like ping-pong balls. One subject to another. Yet somehow for us it works because we always make a full circle. So, tell me what is it about right now."

Knowing she was right, he let the first comment slide. He'd work back to the little girl, but he couldn't talk about E yet. He needed to just embrace the moment. "Having you in my arms, I know this is where we're supposed to be. Maybe not in Ireland, but us together, that's what this is all about. Jack might be angry at first but he's going to realize I'd never let anything happen to you."

"You've always been my protector."

"And you've always been my supporting angel. In the darkest times, you've shined a light on me and gave me the strength I needed to get through it."

Minutes ticked by silently as they just enjoyed each other's company. With them there was no uncomfortable silence. They could remain in silence, or they could talk for hours. There was nothing they couldn't share with each other.

"Annie knows." She tipped her head up to look at him. "I mean, she knows I've always had a thing for you. I've never confirmed it or anything, but she knows."

"I suspected my cousin had an idea." He ran his hand down her back. "She gave me the hotel information for you. She might not have realized I was going to come after you, but she figured I'd contact you."

"Then I'll make you a deal." She propped herself up on her elbow and stared down at him. "I'll see where this goes on the condition that I get to tell Annie, but you deal with Jack."

"I'm not sure that sounds fair but for you I'd do it."

CHAPTER FIVE

The room was dark when Joslynn was jerked awake by a noise. Laying there on the bed, she wasn't sure what she heard. It could have been something from the hallway or even one of the hotel rooms on either side. Still, she couldn't shake the feeling something was wrong.

"No!" Chip's tone was angry.

The voice sounded farther away than the other side of the bed and it took her a moment to realize he wasn't next to her. He was in the bathroom. Slipping out of bed, she crept closer to the bathroom door. She wasn't sure who he was talking to but hearing him so upset made her want to go to him.

"Stay the fuck away from her." Even with Chip keeping his voice low she could hear the growl of anger. "I'm not someone you want to mess with."

With no other voices it was clear he was on the phone with someone, but who? Her first thought was Sal. She glanced over at end table near the sofa and from the light coming in the window she could see her phone still sitting there. That meant it wasn't Sal. He didn't have Chip's number; in fact, he despised her friendship with Chip and had practically forbidden it.

That should have been the first clue he wasn't the right man for her. But, rather than put her foot down, she'd concealed her friendship with Chip. How she would have done that once they got married, she wasn't sure. *I never intended to go through with it.* As the thought crossed her mind, she sucked in a breath and backed away from the bathroom door. Was it true? Had she not intended to go through with it? Thinking back on all the little things, she realized that part of her had already decided she couldn't marry Sal. She just hadn't known how to break it off. That was until he hit her.

Her back brushed against the wall, reminding her of the wall she had built between herself and Sal. That was the only way she got through their relationship. There was no romance, love, or hell, anything like that. She'd stuck with him because her boss demanded it. If Sal didn't give his father good reports on her, she'd be out a job. It wasn't her dream job, but it was a stepping stone to one, so she needed to leave on good terms.

"So much for that." She shook her head. "Why did I even board the plane? I knew it was going to be a disaster."

From the moment Sal had picked her up at her apartment things had gotten off on the wrong foot. *"I don't know why you live in such a dump and with that stupid bitch."* Those had been the first words Sal had said to her as she slid into the backseat of the chauffeured car. She'd wanted to defend Annie, but past experiences had proved to her that only made things worse. Sal didn't like anyone who disagreed with him, especially not her. To him, she was just an extension of him. She didn't have a say in how things happened.

"Why didn't I heed the warnings?" Even as she'd boarded the plane, she knew the trip was going to be a catastrophe, but she'd never pictured getting fired and being left in a different country without a way home.

Every day that passed in Ireland, the worse the situation got. It was as if, without Sal's father to hold the reins, Sal's temper had grown out of control. That was until their final fight, which had proved to her just what he'd wanted her around for. *These negotiations are stressful. I brought you for sex. Otherwise, what do I need*

His words played through her thoughts again, making her stomach churn. How could she have been so blind to his motives? Even more than that, she continued to play over every conversation she'd had with him, trying to reason why she hadn't seen the monster within him before. It was clear to her and anyone who knew Sal that he was mean-spirited and at times evil, but she'd never thought he'd go as far as he did.

The bathroom door opened, spilling light into the room. "Jos, what's wrong?" Chip crossed the space and wrapped his arms around her.

"How didn't I know? Why couldn't I see what kind of person he was? Annie warned me there was something about Sal, something evil, but I couldn't see what she saw. Why?" Her legs gave out but instead of letting her crumble to the floor, he scooped her up into his arms and carried her back to the bed.

"Shh, angel." He laid her on the bed and before joining her, he sat his phone on the nightstand.

"Who were you talking to?"

"Angel." His voice was soft but there was a touch of warning to it as if cautioning her that she wouldn't like the answer.

"Tell me."

"Sal." He tugged the blanket up around them and pulled her tight against him.

"What? How did he get your number?" She tried to pull out of his embrace to sit up, but he held her tight.

"I don't know how for sure, but that doesn't matter. I'll deal with him but in order to do that, I need you to be open with me. He said something— something I need you to clarify."

The moment the words left his mouth, she knew exactly what he meant. Unable to just lie there in his arms, she pulled back from him and sat up. Then, trying to chase the chill that had settled over her away, she hugged the blanket to her chest.

"Jos…"

"Don't. It's not important." She couldn't get enough air into her lungs and the words came out softer than she intended.

"You're important and so is this." He placed his hand on her shoulder. "I'd wait for you to tell me on your own but if I'm understanding what he said the way I think, then someone else is at risk."

She twisted around to look at him. "No…he…oh, Kathy!"

"Tell me." He pressed.

"He brought me with him for sex." Her fingers tightened on the blanket. "Not just for him but for any of them."

"Fucking asshole!" He scooted closer to her and wrapped his arm around her. "I'm going to keep you safe."

"I've got to go back. I've got to…"

"No." His tone left no room for arguing but she was prepared to fight.

"Kathy's just a child. Eighteen. Her parents didn't want her to come, but we needed someone to help prepare the papers. I promised her parents she'd be okay, that I'd be there."

"I've got a friend here in Dublin. He's a Garda—the police force here in Ireland. Let me talk to him and we'll put together a plan. We'll make sure she's safe, but not by you risking yourself. I won't have it."

"She's my responsibility."

"No." He leaned forward so she could see his face. "She's an adult. We'll make this right and while we do, we'll bring down that asshole."

"His father's money will get him out of any trouble he ends up in."

"We'll see about that." He pressed his lips to her temple. "I'm going to give my friend a call."

"Okay." She scooted back against the headboard, pulling the blanket with her.

"Are you okay?"

"Yeah." She glanced over at him as if trying to reassure him. She was anything but okay but if he stayed in bed with her, like she wanted, it could mean Kathy's safety was at risk. She wouldn't risk the young girl for a few minutes of security in Chip's embrace. "Go on, call him."

After a brief hesitation, Chip rose from the bed and grabbed his cell phone again. By the time his friend answered, she was already drifting back to her last conversation with Sal.

"Remember what my father said before we left. You'll play your part completely, otherwise you're finished." Sal stood by the in-room bar, his fourth alcohol drink in hand. "Keeping your job requires my stamp of approval at the end of this trip."

"Play my part!" Livid, she couldn't stop herself from screaming. "I'm here as your assistant, not as a hooker."

"You'll assist me in closing the deal." He brought the drink to his lips and took a long sip. "That is your purpose here."

"You need to get reacquired with the definition of a personal assistant. I can assure you that there isn't a line in my job description that says I must lie on my back for whoever you deem necessary. You can't pass me around like a toy you've gotten tired with. I'm supposed to be your fiancée!"

"As such, you should do whatever it takes to make the family business successful." Polishing off the drink, he grabbed another bottle and staggered toward the sofa. "Otherwise I might have to honor someone else with my attention. Perhaps…Kathy…yeah, she's a bright young child. A little sheltered, but I'm sure she'll do whatever it takes to please me."

CHAPTER SIX

It took Chip a little more than an hour to get things taken care of and now there was nothing to do but wait. His friend, O'Connor, had said he'd check into it and Chip knew he'd do whatever could be done. Meanwhile, he also had a friend back in Pittsburgh looking into Sal's personal life. Had there been other women before Jos that he'd tried prostitute? Were there other victims of Sal's unorthodox business practices?

Whatever happened here in Ireland, Chip was determined to see that Sal would be unable to continue his ways once he returned to the States. His father's money and influence only went so far. Thankfully, Chip's family had connections as well. He'd call in whatever favors he needed to make sure Sal stayed away from Jos and that he wouldn't be a threat to other women.

Turning back to the bed, he wasn't surprised to find Jos still leaning against the headboard. Her mind seemed to be somewhere else as she stared down at her hands. It made him want to do something to take her mind off it. Actually, he wanted to assure her everything would work out. However, that wasn't the kind of relationship they had. They never lied to each other. He could distract her, but he couldn't lie to her.

"Sweet angel." Slipping his phone into the pocket of his jeans that he'd tugged on after he got out of bed, he crossed the room to stand next to her. "O'Connor is checking into it and will make contact with Kathy. He's going to speak with her privately and give her my cell phone number. If she needs help, she can contact us. If there's any reason she doesn't feel comfortable, I've made it clear to O'Connor, we'll meet her somewhere and she can fly home with us."

"I need to go see her. I need to make sure she's okay."

"I figured you'd say that." He sat on the edge of the bed and reached over to take her hand in his. "We need to wait until he talks to her. After that, we'll see what we can do."

"What if he's——"

"No." Gently, he squeezed her hand. "You can't think like that. From what you've told me, she's got a good head on her shoulders. She and her parents obviously trust you enough to allow her to make this trip so I'm positive, if he's made any advances toward her, she'd have called you."

"I thought about calling her, but if he was just talking out his ass it would put her in danger."

"Let O'Connor talk to Kathy and once he does, he'll give me a call. Just hold on a little longer." He glanced toward the window. The first rays of sunlight started peeking over the horizon. "It's early but I don't think either of are going to get anymore sleep. Why don't we go get some breakfast and pick up whatever you need to hold you over until we fly home tomorrow?"

"A shopping trip?" Her lips curled into a halfhearted smile. "Now I know you're trying to distract me. You hate shopping."

"Not with you." He shot her a smile of his own. "Every year when the four of us would go Christmas shopping, we always had a blast. We'd stroll around, hitting every store until we found everything on our lists, plus gag gifts for Jack and Annie. I loved those times and I've missed them."

"Now that you're home and…everything, maybe we can do it this year.

Christmas isn't too far away."

"Everything?" He arched a questioning eyebrow at her. "You mean, us? 'Cause let me tell you, if I'm telling Jack, there's no backing out. We're in this to win. I want my prize."

"Distracting me is working." She rose up onto her knees and scooted closer to him. "Kiss me."

Before he could say anything, she made the first move pressing her lips to his. That was all he needed. He wrapped his hand around her nape, drawing her closer, while a deep groan escaped his throat.

They'd known each other their whole lives, yet, one day, he woke up and saw her in a different light. In that moment, she went from being one of his best friends to the woman he wanted in his bed. It wasn't until he woke up in the hospital, with her sitting by his bedside holding his hand that he realized she had almost slipped away. He couldn't allow that to happen again.

"Jos…" He pulled back, fighting every cell of his body that wanted to continue what they had started. "We've got to stop."

"Why?" Her voice was soft, her eyes wide. "I want this. I want you, now."

"Damn, I love when you're demanding." With his hand still on the back of her neck, he leaned forward, pressing his forehead against hers.

"Last night I was so lost in my own mind, I needed the comfort. Today, I'm not. Yes, I'm worried for Kathy, but that isn't why I'm doing this. I want this. I want you. I want you to make love to me."

"Jos." He brought his hand around to cup her cheek. "I want this too, more than you know, but there's no going back from it."

"I know." Her gaze locked onto his. "Trust me, I've given it a great deal of thought, but we want this. Annie and Jack will come around. They'll see what we have is real. If anyone has a chance to make this work, I think it's us. We're good together."

"When did you give it a thought?"

"Last night, cuddled with you." She ran her hands along his bare chest. "It felt right. I mean it always has, except last night was different. It became clear it wasn't just me who wanted more. The years of flirting and teasing finally came to a head. There's no going back from that. No pretending that we can go back to being friends, not when we both know we want more."

"I'm not saying we can pretend nothing happened and remain friends. Still, there's no rush. We'll take this at whatever pace you want."

"Well…" Her fingers hooked on the waistband of his jeans, quickly finding the button and undoing it. "My pace…"

"Jos." Her name came out edgier than he'd planned, but with her hand so close to his cock, his mind was shutting down.

"You've always considered every possible outcome, overthinking every decision, but this time there's no need. We know each other inside and out. This is right. We're right together."

He wasn't sure if it was her words or his brain sending up the white flag in surrender, but he rose from the bed and stripped off his jeans before sliding back beside her. "Come here."

She scooted closer, pressing her body against his side, but he wanted more. Grabbing a hold of her hips, he pulled her up onto him so she was arched over him. His cock stood at full attention, brushing along her stomach.

"Touch me." Though he had a preferred spot, it didn't matter where she touched him; he just needed her hands on him.

As if she could read his thoughts, she wrapped her hands around his cock, gently working her way up and down his length.

"Shit, woman." Her light touch was like all of the years he'd waited for her piled up on him, making his need to claim her nearly overwhelming. It was tempting to roll her over on the bed and push his cock into her, without giving her another second to reconsider.

"You've got too many clothes on." He grabbed hold of the hem of the T-shirt he'd given her to sleep in and tugged upwards. His breath escaped him as her naked body came into view. She had been naked under his shirt. If he had known that hours before when she'd come out of the bathroom wearing it, he wasn't sure he could have stopped himself from easing the thin material up her gorgeous body.

"Like what you see?" she teased, giving his cock a slight squeeze.

Pulling his gaze away from her naked body, he forced himself to look up at her. "When the four of us rented the cabin at the lake right before I deployed, you wore a little black bikini on our last day there and that image burned into my mind. You were beautiful. The only thing that kept me from untying those thin strings and stripping the flimsy material off you was Jack's presence. Even that has nothing on this moment. So beautiful." He slid his hands up her hips, working his way up the length of her torso. As his thumbs brushed along the underside of her breasts, she jerked, her eyes closing. Keeping his gaze on her face, he rubbed his thumbs along her areola, drawing small circles until he reached her nipples. As he teased the hard nipple, her back arched, and she pressed her stomach against his cock.

"I need you inside me." Her voice was husky and full of need.

"Rise up."

Her eyelids popped open. "Chip, who's always in control, is handing over the reins?"

"Don't get used to it. It's temporary." Part of this was to make sure she wanted whatever happened, no second thoughts, but the other part was a more selfish reason. He wanted to see her body over his, her breasts bouncing as she rode his cock.

Without wasting another second, she rose up onto her knees and arched over his shaft. The need for him to grab her hips and ease her down on him was overwhelming but he kept his hands on her breasts. He told her that it would be at her pace and he meant that. At least for now.

She guided his cock inside her. Every inch she moved down his length made his hunger for her that much stronger. It seemed to be agonizingly slow as she worked him inside her.

Unable to help himself, he took hold of her hips, bringing her completely down on him—buried to the hilt. He thought the need to ravish her would subside, but it only grew stronger.

"Please, Chip."

He kept his hands on her hips, helping her work his shaft up and down. Slowly at first, but as she began to feel comfortable, she found the pace and continued to drive herself up and down, going faster with each pump.

With her in control, he moved his hands away from her hips, sliding them along her body. Watching as her breasts bounced with each pump, he reached up to claim them. His fingers slid over the hard buds of her nipples, teasing them again. He had the urge to arch up into her, to speed their pace, but he didn't want to throw her off her game.

Her inner muscles tightened around him until he thought he was going to lose it. She sped her pace until she was nearly slamming herself onto him. Tipping her head back, she closed her eyes as she continued to propel herself up and down while he met her with thrusts of his own.

His hands returned to her hips as they matched thrust for thrust. With each stroke, the fire within him burned brighter and hotter. His climax loomed in the distance, but he wanted to see her release before he would allow himself the pleasure. He wanted to see her eyes gloss over and the utter joy as she climaxed around his shaft.

"Oh, Chip!" she cried out, her head tipped back, her voice tight and full of need. "Don't stop." She held onto him for all it was worth, riding his thrusts, then leaned forward, her breasts jiggling with each movement, just out of reach of his mouth, taunting him. At last, her body tightened around him. She was nearly there.

"Look at me," he demanded.

She opened her eyes, but it wasn't like she was truly seeing him. A glaze within their depths suggested she wasn't completely there but feeling the effects of her oncoming climax. "Faster!"

She slammed down into him as he arched up to meet her, driving the force of each pump. He thrust deeper and faster into a perfect rhythm. "Yes! Chip!" she moaned.

Her muscles squeezed tight around him, the final act he needed to find his own release. Breathless, she leaned forward, her body pressed against his chest, while he stayed buried deep within her. Needing to see her, he brushed her hair from her face. As if understanding what he wanted, she tipped her head to look up at him, her eyes glossy and dreamy—the aftermath of amazing sex. He had fanaticized about this moment for years, but that fantasy had been nothing like the actual act.

"That was better than in my dreams." She slid off him and curled against his body.

"You're telling me." He wrapped his arm around her and held her close. "I'm never going to get enough of you. I love you, Jos."

"I love you too." Her eyelids drifted closed as her fingers played down along his chest.

He looped his arms around her, keeping her tight against him. This was the moment he had figured would be the end of one relationship and the beginning of another. Instead it felt more like a continuance—as if moving from one chapter to another. No break, just a perfect, smooth transition.

CHAPTER SEVEN

The day sped by quicker than Joslynn ever expected as they waited for any word from O'Connor. Chip's phone had gone off several times, but each time it had been with information from his buddy in Pittsburgh. By three o'clock, her anxiety was starting to grow and nothing Chip could do was easing it. Grabbing her phone, she thought again about calling Kathy. Instead, an unanswered call caught her attention.

They hadn't left the room and her phone had been at arm's length the whole time. How had she missed a call? The only time she could think of was that the call had come through during her shower. She'd expected to shower alone, but Chip had joined her, quickly changing the plans for a quick shower to shower sex.

Looking down at the screen, she recognized the number. It was Mr. Esposito—Sal's father.

"Chip." She glanced over at him where he worked on her laptop. "He called."

Rising from his chair at the small table, Chip crossed over to sit next to her on the bed. "Put it on speaker and play it."

She didn't want to hear what Mr. Esposito had to say but the message might hold something that could help them, so she pressed play.

"Our talk before the trip must have fallen on deaf ears. You're under direct orders to follow every order given to you. Sal's willing to give you another chance, but I'm not as lenient. If you're not back at the hotel by three, he'll proceed without you and the girl will take your place. This business is too important to let some selfish bitch destroy all we've worked for. Three o'clock or consider yourself fired and all contracts breached and voided."

She dropped the phone onto the bed before she ended up throwing it across the room and rose from the bed. That asshole thought he could just order her to sleep with strangers and she'd do it. She might have been eager about the job, wanting to prove she could make it at a fast-paced firm, but it wasn't worth her self-worth. Even if Chip hadn't shown up in Ireland when he did, she wouldn't have gone back to the hotel. She'd have found another way.

"It's two-forty." She dragged her hand through her hair, trying to determine if there was something she could do to save Kathy.

"You're not thinking about going back, are you?" Chip came to stand next to her.

"No." She turned to him. "Why haven't we heard from O'Connor? What is he doing?"

"I don't know but I'm going to call him about the message. It's clear he's talking about Kathy." He pressed his lips to the top of her head.

Before she could say anything, his cell phone vibrated next to the laptop, catching their attention. "Maybe that's O'Connor now."

She could at least hope and with a little extra luck, he might have some good news, too.

Chip stepped away from her and went to the table. As she watched him, her own phone buzzed, alerting her to a text message. Pulling her gaze from him, she wandered toward the bed, expecting to find a message from Annie.

As she looked down at the screen, she was surprised to find Sal's name above the message. *Fucking bitch. Without an offering, I'll lose this contract. If you're not here in ten minutes, I'm coming for you. I know you're with that freak.*

"Chip." Since she hadn't been listening, she didn't know who he was talking to, but whoever it was could wait. He needed to see this. At least he needed to know about the threat; she didn't want him to see the freak part. Sal had always called him degrading names like that, but to her, Chip wasn't anything like Sal claimed.

"O'Connor, hold on a sec." Chip tipped the phone away from his mouth. "Jos, what's wrong?"

"If I'm not at Sal's hotel room in ten minutes, he's coming here."

Chip pulled her close and grabbed her phone from her hand, reading the text message. So much for trying to protect his feelings. Luckily, seeing the whole thing didn't seem to faze him. "O'Connor, we got another communication, this time from Sal."

"Where's Kathy?" She looked up at him. If Sal was freaking out, that had to mean Kathy was gone. Was she safe?

"O'Connor has her at the station. It took longer to locate her, which is why we haven't heard from him. She called home and her father has a ticket on a flight for her this evening. One of the officers will escort her to the gate and make sure she gets on the plane safely," he assured her.

"I'm in the lobby." O'Connor's voice came through the phone's speaker.

Catching a glimpse of herself in the mirror, she realized she was still only wearing his T-shirt. She pulled away from Chip as he ended the call and glanced around the room for her jeans. "Need to get dressed."

"Damn right. No one gets to see your beautiful body, except me." He tipped his head toward the chair where her clothes lay. "Throw on your jeans, but keep my shirt on. I love how it looks on you."

"You just like that he'll know I'm yours if I'm wearing our shirt," she teased, tugging on her jeans. "Do you think Sal will…" She let her words trail off. Sal was an asshole used to getting his way. If this was what he wanted, he'd go to any length to get it. Even coming after her. He'd never learned to face consequences for his actions. In the past, she'd thought it was because his father was trying to make up for not being there when Sal was young. Now she realized they were one and the same. Mr. Esposito knew what Sal was going and supported it. She wasn't sure if the older man had done the same things, but she wouldn't put it past him. The recent events had been enough to show her what a sleaze ball she'd been working for.

"How have I been so blind? I should have seen what kind of men I was working for—what kind of man I agreed to marry. Part of me knew Dad wouldn't approve of Sal. It's why I've been holding off taking him to meet my parents. I just never realized it was this bad."

"Jack voiced his concerns about why you were hiding this man away from the family." She turned back to the bed to find Chip sitting on the edge, lacing up his boots. "It was unlike you to keep something like this from Jack. He was concerned for you. Especially since whenever he mentioned Sal, you'd change the subject."

"I didn't." She thought back to the conversations she'd had with her brother. "Shit. I didn't realize I was."

A knock at the door had Chip stand, his body stiff, fists clenched. Just by looking at him she could see the change in his demeanor. He no longer looked relaxed, but on guard. It was likely O'Connor was at the door, but on the off chance it was Sal, Chip would be ready. The question was, would she be?

Twenty minutes of Jos pacing the hotel room had Chip ready to bust. He needed to ease the tension within her but with them stuck in the room with O'Connor there was little he could do to distract her. Seeing her wound so tight made him edgy. It was a new experience for him. Anytime he had gone on a mission there was a game plan; he knew what their mission was and what steps they'd take to accomplish it. Now he had to wait for Sal to make the first move. There wasn't enough evidence or crime for the Garda to arrest Sal. If he attacked or tried to kidnap Joslynn, that would be enough for O'Connor and the other Garda stationed around the hotel to take him into custody.

"He should be here by now." Jos glanced out the window again.

"Maybe he's all talk." Chip leaned against the wall, watching the door, expecting a knock at any moment.

O'Connor stepped away from the door where he'd been talking on the phone in hushed whispers. "He's rabbited. Caught sight of one of my guys."

"What?" Jos snapped.

"I've got guys tracking him." O'Connor slipped his phone back into his pocket. "I need to get out there. I'll be in touch. If you can get an earlier flight back to the States, take it. We've set up an alert on his name, so if he'd try to check in at the airport, we'd be notified. I can assure you he's not leaving the country tonight."

"I'll call the airlines and see what can be done." Chip moved away from the wall and held out his hand to O'Connor. "Thanks, man. I appreciate your help."

"Anytime. Next time you're in my homeland, let it be under better circumstances." O'Connor shook his hand and glanced toward her. "Madam, it was a pleasure meeting you."

"You, too." She paused by the window as Chip saw O'Connor out.

"Jos." Chip came up behind her, resting his hand on her shoulder. "This isn't over."

"It should have been." She leaned back against his chest. "This should have been a simple operation that ended with him in cuffs. Now who knows where he is?"

"Maybe it's better this way. Now we can deal with him back in Pittsburgh.

Turns out they already have a warrant for his arrest." He spun her around to face him.

"Arrest warrant? For what?" Her eyes widened as she stared at him.

"Attempted murder." His hands slid down her arms, comforting her. "There's a woman who had a similar experience with him a couple of months ago. When she refused to do what he wanted, he tried to kill her."

"Months ago. Why is this just coming out now?"

"She's been in a coma since it happened, and woke up only a few days ago. I don't know all the details, but we can find out when we get home. What I'm trying to say is, Mr. Esposito isn't going to be able to make these charges go away." He pulled her against his body and wrapped his arms snug around her. "This will be over soon and he'll never hurt you, Kathy, or anyone else again."

CHAPTER EIGHT

The whole way home, Joslynn kept reminding herself that everything would work out. She was finally on her way home and Kathy should already be back with her parents. She'd follow up with the young girl in the coming days, but knowing she'd be surrounded by family was a weight off Joslynn's shoulders.

Yet, knowing they'd left behind Sal in Ireland didn't ease the tension within her. The nagging feeling that something was off was still eating away at her. Maybe it wasn't about Sal. Maybe it was the fact they were going home and she'd have to tell Annie what had happened with Chip. Eventually, she'd have to tell Jack, too. At least, with him deployed, she didn't have to face that when she got off the plane, too.

"Jos." Chip's voice pulled her out of her thoughts and back into the present.

"Yeah?" Snuggled against his side, she tipped her head to glance up at him.

"Talk to me?"

She pulled back enough so she could take him in completely. He wasn't a fan of flying but after takeoff he relaxed, as long as the flight remained smooth. His words made her wonder if he was becoming anxious knowing they'd be coming into Pittsburgh International Airport soon. But, as she looked up at him, she found him calm.

"You've been lost in your thoughts. Are you okay?" he added as if understanding why she was staring up at him.

"I was just thinking about everything that's happened." She took his other hand in hers and linked their fingers. "Everything seemed dismal before you found me in that pub and now, even knowing Sal is out there somewhere, I can't help but feel a little carefree. Well, maybe that's not the word. I'm still concerned about telling Annie and Jack but being here with you is worth it."

"Annie still thinks we're coming home tomorrow. Why don't we go back to my house and face her tomorrow?"

As much as she wanted to go home and get into her own clothes, rather than remain in this outfit she'd picked up at one of the shops near the hotel, she'd rather spend the night with him. "Okay."

"Ladies and gentlemen, if you could return to your seats, we'll begin our decent momentarily." The captain's voice came out the loudspeaker, causing Chip's body to tighten.

"Hey." She squeezed his hand. "We'll be on the ground in a few minutes."

"I know." His tone was clipped but his gaze stayed locked on hers. "I'm looking forward to getting you back to my place."

"Really now?" Teasing, she raised an eyebrow at him.

"You don't know how many nights I've dreamt about having you in my bed." He tangled his fingers in her long hair, tugging gently. "I bought that house with you in mind. When I was house hunting my realtor took me through it and I knew you'd love it. I could picture you in every space of that house and without thinking twice, I made an offer."

"I wondered why you purchased it. You were looking for a condo near the city, so you could enjoy the views. Instead, you purchased a rural ranch. It was so unlike you. Annie even joked it was more my style than yours."

"I didn't think we'd ever get to this stage, but here we are."

"Why?" The question came out more like a whisper. "Why did we wait so long?"

"Fear of rejection, fear of risking our friendship, the knowledge you deserve someone better, Annie and Jack. Take your pick, angel."

"There's no one better than you." She brought her hand up to cup the side of his face. "Every man I met I've always compared to you. Every single one of them fell short."

"I—"

"Don't." She brought her finger to his lips. "I know what you're going to say, but you're wrong. Your burns mean nothing. Your tendency to shut yourself away also means nothing to me. You know I prefer a quiet night home than going out. You also know I'm hesitant to let anyone new into my close group of friends. Some say I'm shut off, and that's fine 'cause it works for me. I hold those I care about close and they're the people that matter. Everything else is just window dressing."

"Which makes me love you even more." He sucked her finger between his lips and dragged his teeth along it. "With you I don't have to pretend I'm someone else. You know me inside and out."

She loved the way his mouth worked, his tongue teasing along her finger. It made her want to find somewhere private and soon. Leaning in close, she pressed her mouth close to his ear. "Keep that up and I'm going to want to see just what that mouth can do."

"Angel, I'll have you screaming my name so loud, you'll be glad I chose a rural place. Otherwise you'd be too embarrassed to ever set foot outside again." He took her hand from his face and brought it down into his lap. "Feel that. That's what you do to me."

"You have me all to yourself. There's no one else I'd rather be with." Through his jeans, she cupped his cock in her hand. "I'm going to take care of this and since I'm now unemployed, I have all the time in the world. At least until

49

I find another job."

As the plane touched down, his lips curled into a smile. "Without any luggage, we should be at my place in twenty minutes."

She ran her hand down his length one last time. "The sooner the better."

They made it back to Chip's house in record time and, considering how her hand on his thigh continued to brush along the length of his cock, that was a good thing. Otherwise, he might have had to find a dark place on the side of the road to get another taste of Jos. She made him feel like a teenager again, constantly on edge with need. Every cell within his body seemed to yearn for another touch of her but more than that, he wasn't sure if he'd ever get enough of her.

"Chip…" Her voice was husky as he pushed open the front door. "I need you."

He glanced over his shoulder as she tugged the T-shirt she was wearing over her head. "Fuck, Jos." He wrapped his arm around her bare midsection and tugged her into the house. It had nothing to do with the fact she was standing on his porch in only a bra and jeans. Rather, it was his uncontrollable desire. He wanted to push her against the wall in the entryway and have his way with her.

Her fingers went to the top of his jeans, tugging on the hem slightly as she tried to get the button to pop open. "That was the longest plane ride of my life."

"It was nothing like the one I took coming to find you. Every second seemed like hours as I fought to keep myself in my seat. I've never been one to sit and wait well but knowing you were in danger was my breaking point." Even as he spoke, he slid his hand under her hair and unhooked her bra. He needed to see her perky breasts with her hard nipples waiting for his lips to claim them. As the material slid down her arms, he wasn't disappointed.

"Bedroom, naked, now," he said gruffly.

"Coming." She slipped passed him, her hands already working on the clasp of her own jeans.

"I'll be there in a minute. Need to let J.J. in."

"Oh, J.J." Her face lit up at the mention of the pup.

"Later. First I get your attention, then you can love on the furball." Wanting nothing more than to follow her, he forced himself to head toward the back porch and his—no doubt—anxious German Shepherd. A week after he'd returned home J.J. had showed up on his porch, a skinny pup who, from the condition of his coat, had been on his own for a while. They found solace in each other and the pup had given him companionship that he had been lacking since his discharge from the military.

"Meany," she complained but instead of following him, she headed back toward the bedroom.

He waited until he heard the bedroom door close behind her to open the sliding glass door that led to the closed in porch. J.J. stood at the door, waiting to be allowed in. His tail thumping off the porch.

"Hey, pup." He reached down, giving him a scratch between the ears. "Come on inside."

J.J. barked before stepping inside and jumping up to put his front paws on Chip's chest.

"Down." Even as he gave the order, he couldn't fault the pup for being excited he was home. "Mr. Mason and his boys came over and gave you plenty of attention while I was gone. So, go lie down. Later, Jos will give you all the attention your heart could desire." His lips curled into a smile, thinking about the two of them together, roughhousing on the floor or cuddled up on the sofa. They were everything to him. The two of them completed him in every way.

With J.J. inside, he locked the porch door and headed toward the back of the house where he'd find Jos, hopefully naked and spread out on his bed. As he made his way to the bedroom, he scanned through the rooms. Routine, nothing more. J.J. would have alerted him if anyone was in the house.

Finally, he pushed open the bedroom door and found her spread out on the bed just as he expected it. Only, the actual image was much better than anything his fantasies could create. Her beautiful, long, dark brown hair spread across the white pillow cases. Her nipples stood tall like a beacon welcoming him home.

"So fucking beautiful."

CHAPTER NINE

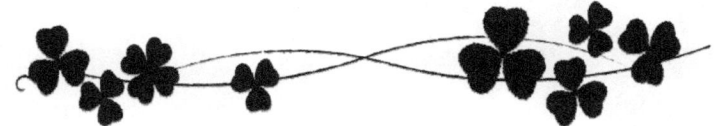

"What are you waiting for?" She ran her hand over her breast and down her stomach.

Not needing any further encouragement, he slipped out of his clothes, dropping them onto the floor, and climbed into bed next to her. He trailed his hand down her body and between her thighs. The caresses of his fingers had her spreading her legs, and her breath caught in her chest. He explored up her inner thigh, ever so slowly, until he slipped his finger between her folds, quickly finding her center and working deep within her. His thumb brushed along her clit, sending fire through her body.

"Fuck, Jos. A few caresses and you're ready for me. I love the way your body responds to me."

The ability to speak was gone, leaving her unable to respond to him. A moan tore from her as he worked a second finger into her. In and out, quicker with every pump. As her climax approached, he slowed, until he stopped altogether.

"Chip, I need you." Her hands were on his sides. As her fingers trailed along the scars from his burns, their eyes met. "Don't pull away from me."

"I'm not."

"Bullshit." She continued to slowly rub along every burn, taking her time with the deeper ones. "I saw the shift in your eyes, the slight way your body jerked as you wanted to pull away from my touch."

"I didn't." He leaned forward, pressing his forehead to hers. "It's an instinctive reaction, but I didn't really mean to send that message. Most people don't even want to look at them, but they don't seem to bother you. You touch them. It's something I'm not used to."

"Does it bother you when I touch you there?" Not sure whether to continue or not, she stopped.

"No." He lifted his head from hers. "To be honest, the nerve endings have changed underneath my burns. They are…"

"What?" she pressed when his words trailed off.

"More alive. I guess that's the best way to describe them. Maybe it's just your touch, I don't know, because I keep them hidden from most people. Your simple caresses feel on the verge of tickling, yet they seem to spark a fire within me. It's hard to explain but I like it."

That was enough to allow her to continue on the path she had chosen, letting her fingers dance along the sides of him. As if that put him back on track, he slid down her body, blazing a trail of kisses across her stomach and stroking along her curves. With every touch, she arched her hips into him, demanding more. Her nails dug in just enough to bite into the skin. "I love when you do that. Your nails leave crescent moon shapes on my skin, as if trying to mark the moments of pleasure we've shared."

"Permanent reminders of our love." Her lips curled into a smile.

"Don't worry, angel. There's no going back from this. We'll be able to make new marks whenever the previous ones fade."

His thumb brushed along her clit, stealing any comment she might have made. Her hips lifted from the bed, arching against his chest. She pressed against his hand, keeping it there as her body rocked back and forth, demanding a faster pace. "Please, Chip!"

"Faster? Slower? Stop?" He stopped moving and even though she was still wiggling against his hand, it wasn't the same. He knew just where to touch her to make her melt.

"Asshole!" She growled at him, hating him for denying her what her body needed so badly.

"Well, then." His thumb brushed along her clit one final time before he pulled his hand away from her.

Shocked by the loss of his touch, she opened her eyes, only to find him grinning down at her. The cocky grin stretched across his face made her wish she had the willpower to get up. She'd go play with J.J. and leave him without sex. But, she wanted this as badly as he did, if not more. They both might be able to get themselves off but it wouldn't be the same. "I should leave you to your own devices now."

"But?" He arched over her, waiting for her to finish her thought.

"Damn you." With a smile tugging at the corners of her lips, she lightly pushed against his chest. "I want this. I need your touch, your…"

"My what?"

"I need you inside me." She reached between them and wrapped her fingers around his cock, applying just enough pressure to force a moan from him, but not so much as to hurt. "Unless you want the worst case of blue balls in your life, you'll give me what I need."

"It seems as though I've had a case of blue balls since we were teenagers and I realized you were mine."

"I love it when you say that. I can hear the claim in the way you growl the word 'mine'. It's so sexy."

"You *are* mine. You've always been, and you always will be." He trailed a hand down her body. "I'll prove it again now as we break this bed in properly and I fuck you until you can't walk straight."

55

"What are you waiting for?" She leaned back against the pillows, willing him to make his move.

As he slipped into place on top of her, she brought her legs up on either side of him and lazily dragged one hand along the side of his chest. Her fingers teased along his ribs but it was the contour of his muscles that she was enjoying. The tight muscles contracted under her touch, showing off the beauty of his chest. He worked hard to bulk up and she admired it.

His chest vibrated as he chuckled and she looked up at him. "What?"

"I love that look. Your face shines just as it did on Christmas morning when we were kids." He wiggled his hips, teasing the tip of his cock over her opening. "Are you ready for what I'm about to give you?"

"Trust me, I want this. I've wanted to be back in this position since the last time I found myself under you."

He teased the tip of his dick along her slit before he arched forward, shoving it into her pussy in one quick movement, clearly telling her conversation time was over; all he wanted out of her was moans and her screaming his name.

A whimper tore from her chest as her core muscles stretched to accommodate his width. "Chip!" Breathlessly, she ran her hands up his chest and let her body adjust.

Staring down at her, he slowly pumped his hips, sliding his dick in and out of her. Using one arm to keep his position above her, he brought his other hand to her breast. He groaned as his fingers found her hard nipples. Rolling the hardened bud between his fingers, pinching it with enough pressure to have her arching forward, he increased his pace. Each pump of his hips had him going harder and faster, stealing her breath as her climax neared. Heat coiled between her thighs and her sex clenched around him.

"Faster!" She lifted her body up to meet his.

"You feel so fucking good wrapped around my dick." He pulled nearly his full length out, before slamming back into her. When he did, he sped his pace up. Their bodies rocked back and forth, each thrust gaining momentum, drawing her closer to orgasm.

As if knowing she was close but needed more to push her over the edge, he reached between them, his thumb instantly finding her clit. But that wasn't enough for him, so he dipped his head, his lips wrapping around her nipple to suck it in between his teeth. He swirled his tongue around the bud before his teeth closed down around it.

"Yes!" She hissed in a mixture of pain and pleasure. Her climax was almost upon her as she arched forward, sending his dick deeper in her.

"Look at me, Jos. I want your eyes on me. I want you to know it's my dick in you, bringing you to your orgasm." His voice sounded strained as if he were close to his own peak but wouldn't give in until she had her release first.

"Chip," she whispered, her climax within reach. "Faster, please." She raked her nails down his chest.

With one last flick over her clit, he leaned back, placing both hands on her hips, and pounded into her faster. She wrapped her legs around him, locking her ankles together at the small of his back, which kept him from pulling back too far. Tension had her muscles constricting around him as her orgasm neared, urging him to engage an even faster rhythm, and his eyes glazed over with his own ecstasy creeping up on him.

Keeping her gaze locked on him, she pressed her body to his. Her fingers tangled in his longer strands, bringing his head down so she could claim a kiss. Slipping her tongue in between his lips, she moaned his name as her release found her. With her free hand, she raked the skin along his chest, digging her nails into his flesh.

Her core muscles tightened around him and she could feel the tension release from him as he slammed into her one final time before leaning forward against her and letting go, filling her. He buried his face in the arch of her shoulder. "Fuck, Jos."

"Mmm…now I know I can't ever let you go." With her fingers still in his hair, she let the palm of her hand brush along the side of his face. Her muscles continued to tighten around him, milking his cock for every drop. "I love you, Chip."

"I've always known once I claimed you that I could never let you go." He tipped his head down to the curve of her shoulder and growled. "Mine."

Wiggling against him, she dragged her hands lazily along his sides.

"Keep wiggling and I'm going to have you moaning again in no time." He slipped out of her and collapsed next to her, before bringing her body snug against his. "I love you, Joslynn Ashburn, more than I could ever put into words."

CHAPTER TEN

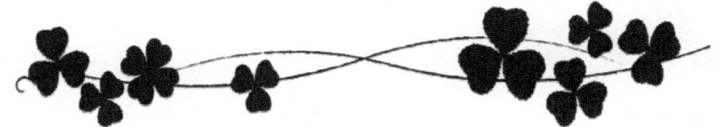

Wearing one of Chip's old shirts, Joslynn sat on the floor, rubbing J.J.'s stomach, while he stood near the kitchen bar, watching them. Was it wrong of him to be jealous of the pup? He wanted to pick her up and carry her back to the bedroom so that her hands would land on him, not on the dog. He was never going to get enough of her.

Unable to stop himself, he sat his beer down and crossed the space between them. "Jos."

"Yeah?" Tipping her head back to look up at him, he could see her own desire peeking through her dark brown eyes.

"Come shower with me." He held out his hand to her.

"You just want to get me naked and wet again," she teased, accepting his hand.

"Wet in a different way." J.J. let out a bark, which Chip ignored. He didn't care if the dog was unhappy she was being stolen away. He was alpha of the house and J.J. knew it. He pulled her close and slid his hands under her shirt. "I always want you naked."

"You're insatiable." Even as she said the words, she slipped her hand down the front of his lounge pants and wrapped it around the length of his cock.

"For you, yes." The shirt was nearly to her shoulders when the sound of a key in the door pulled his attention away from the beauty in front of him. J.J. stood, barking, between the door and them. On full alert, he pushed her behind him, moving quickly, with her still tucked behind him, to the gun in the box on the fireplace ledge.

"What's going on?" Her voice was low, but the fear was evident.

"Take J.J. and—" He checked the gun, making sure it was loaded, as the door opened.

J.J. growled, launching toward the figure in the doorway.

"Wow, J.J." a familiar voice called out as the dog pounced.

"Jack?" Even though he thought he recognized the voice, he hadn't lowered the gun from the figure in the doorway.

"Yeah. Now call off your dog."

"J.J.!" Chip hollered, the dog instantly reacting. When J.J. came to stand next to them, Chip lowered the gun. "What the hell are you doing here? You're supposed to be in Iraq."

"I'm on leave. I went to Joslynn's but Annie said she was on a business trip. You were supposed to be out of town, too. She wouldn't tell me what's going on, but she seemed off." Jack stepped into the house and dropped his bag by the door. His eyes widened. "Joslynn? What the fuck is going on?"

"Long story." She stepped out from behind Chip and went to rub on J.J.'s head.

"Are you fucking my sister?" Jack's gaze focused on Chip.

"Woah, now." Joslynn took a step toward her brother, but Chip slipped his hand into hers, stopping her.

"This wasn't how you were supposed to find out."

"Joslynn, get in the car," Jack ordered.

"No." She took a deep breath. "Chip's right. We didn't want you to find out like this…"

"I'm out of the country and you just move in on her? What the hell?" Jack slammed the door behind him. "She's my sister."

"And I'm right here." She snapped. "We're adults. We know what we were doing."

"You're my best friend." Jack still refused to look at her. "My sister."

"None of this was meant to hurt you." She let go of Chip's hand and stepped toward her brother. "Hell, you and Annie are the reason we waited so long."

"Why now?" Jack shook his head. "Fuck, man, I knew you had a thing for her. You never hid it well, but still I never thought you'd go behind my back like this. You betrayed me by keeping this from me."

"It just happened," she said.

"She's right." Chip stepped up behind her, his hand resting on her shoulder. "She was on a business trip with that asshole Sal in Ireland and there was an issue. I went to take care of it and well…"

"You couldn't keep your dick in your pants."

"Stop!" she screamed. "Jack, I knew you'd be upset but think about this. You trust Chip more than anyone—"

"And he does this."

"Let me finish!" she snapped. "You trust him enough to watch your back. You should trust him enough to keep your sister safe. What other person could you have that level of trust with from the beginning? We didn't do this to hurt you."

"Joslynn…" Jack ran his hand over his face before looking at her again. "It's you I'm worried about getting hurt."

"Don't." She reached out and placed her hand on her brother's arm. "Chip loves me, just as I love him. He'd never hurt me."

"I'll fucking kill you if you hurt her." Jack stared past her to Chip.

"Wouldn't expect anything less." Chip nodded. "She means everything to both of us. Are you going to be okay with it?"

"Yeah." Jack nodded.

Chip squeezed her shoulder before stepping back. "Since you're on leave, I'm expecting you'll want to stay here. You know where the guest room is."

"I can stay with my parents." Jack rolled his shoulders. "Kentucky is too far to travel back and forth for this short leave."

"Don't be silly." Joslynn shot him a bright smile. "I want to spend as much time with you as I can. Since I'm unemployed, that won't be a problem. This will be just like old times."

"Except you're sleeping with my best friend." Jack let out a halfhearted laugh.

"Look at the bright side—she's not with that asshole any longer," Chip joked trying his best to ease the tension in the air. "Come sit down. We've got a lot to fill you in on."

"You mean like how there's an arrest warrant out for him?" Jack stared at his sister, shaking his head. "What kind of trouble have you gotten yourself into?"

"I'm taking care of it." He pulled Jos back against him and wrapped his arms around her. "I'm taking care of her. Right, angel?"

"Right." She tipped her head back to look up at him. "It's all going to be fine."

He'd make sure no danger came her way, not for as long as he was alive.

CHAPTER ELEVEN

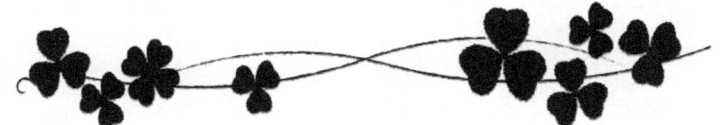

Two weeks had passed since the trip to Ireland and Joslynn couldn't have been happier. Even though she hadn't technically moved out of the condo she shared with Annie, she was mostly living with Chip at his place. She hadn't found a job yet—not that she was actively looking. Since her brother's leave had ended, she'd spent her time with Chip and J.J.

News had come on Jack's last day of leave that Sal had been arrested. The attempted murder case was strong, and it was likely he'd be sentenced to a long stint in prison. Mr. Esposito was pressuring him to take a plea deal to keep it out of the papers as much as possible, but Sal was holding out that his father's influence could get the charges dropped.

With Sal behind bars, it was one less thing she had to worry about. When the news hit, she was worried Mr. Esposito might contact her again, but as of yet, she hadn't heard from him. He had other things to deal with and if she had to guess, he was trying to convince his son's victim to change her story.

With Sal and Mr. Esposito both out of her life, this allowed her to move on with her life without the worry. Everything was coming together and working out better than she could have expected.

"Jos?" Chip stepped out of the sliding door onto the porch. "There you are."

"Were you looking for me?" She gave J.J.'s head a scratch before tapping his butt to make him move off the patio loveseat, giving Chip space to sit.

"Kathy called. She agreed to dinner tomorrow night. She sounds happy. She accepted a new job at a company owned by a friend of her father. We're going to meet her at a restaurant just down the street from her office." He sat down next to her and she quickly adjusted so she could curl up against him.

"My reserved sweetie is going to venture out to dinner," she teased. "Thank you."

"Anything for you." He pressed his lips to the top of her head. "I love you, Jos. Plus, this will prepare me for the social event of the year."

"Social event of the year? What's that?"

"Our wedding." His thumb brushed over the top of her engagement ring. "Might be just a small affair for you, but you know me, I prefer to keep out of the spotlight. I'd rather watch things from afar than be center of attention. However, me being the groom, that's impossible."

"The end result will be worth it."

"Hell, yeah. You'll be Mrs. Chip Olson."

And she couldn't wait.

ABOUT MARISSA AND THOMAS DOBSON

After more than twelve years of marriage and sixty books, Marissa was finally able to convince Thomas to collaborate on a project with her. It went better than either of them expected and there's most likely more coming in the future. Be sure to watch Marissa's website for more details.

www.MarissaDobson.com

ALSO BY MARISSA DOBSON

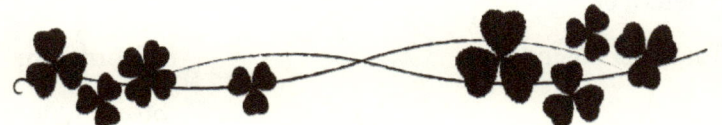

Alaskan Tigers:

Tiger Time

The Tiger's Heart

Tigress for Two

Night with a Tiger

Trusting a Tiger

Alaskan Tigers Box Set Vol. 1

Jinx's Mate

Two for Protection

Bearing Secrets

Tiger Tracks

Healing the Clan

Alaskan Tigers Box Set Vol. 2

Her Black Tiger

Tiger Trouble

Alpha Claimed

Forever Creek Shifters:

Forever's Fight

Protecting Forever

Crimson Hollow:

Romancing the Fox

Loving the Bears

A Lion's Chance

Swift Move

Purrable Lion

Bearly Alive

Saved by a Lion

Furever Mated Box Set

SEALed for You:

Ace in the Hole

Explosive Passion

Operation Family

Marine for You:

Lucky Chance

Back from Hell

A Marine's Second Chance

Tanner Cycles:

Until Sydney

Phantom Security:

Different Sides

Undercover Agent

Takeover Agent

Cedar Grove Medical:

Hope's Toy Chest

Destiny's Wish

Leena's Dream

Cedar Grove Medical Box Set

Beyond Monogamy:

Theirs to Treasure

Fate:

Snowy Fate

Sarah's Fate

Mason's Fate

As Fate Would Have It

Half Moon Harbor Resort:

Learning to Live

Learning What Love Is

Her Cowboy's Heart

Half Moon Harbor Resort Vol. 1

United Homefront Ranch:

Destination Heaven

Reaper:

A Touch of Death

Stormkin:

Storm Queen

Clearwater:

Winterbloom

Unexpected Forever

Losing to Win

Christmas Countdown

The Surrogate

Clearwater Romance Volume One

Small Town Doctor

Stand Alone:

Through Smoke

SEALed Rescue

SEALed in Texas

Starting Over

Secret Valentine

Restoring Love

ALSO BY MARISSA DOBSON & THOMAS DOBSON

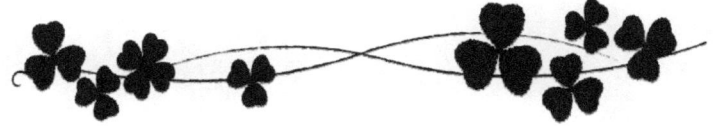

Snowy Peaks

A Wyoming Christmas